Helping Kids Heal

My Baby Sister
Is a Preemie

Written by Diana M. Amadeo

Illustrated by Cheri Bladholm

Zonderkidz

Zonder**kidz**®

The children's group of Zondervan

www.zonderkidz.com

My Baby Sister Is a Preemie
Copyright © 2005 by The Zondervan Corporation
Illustrations copyright © 2005 by Cheri Bladholm

Requests for information should be addressed to:
Zonderkidz, Grand Rapids, Michigan 49530

Library of Congress Cataloging-in-Publication Data

Amadeo, Diana M.
  My baby sister is a preemie / by Diana M. Amadeo ; [illustrations by Cheri Bladholm].-- 1st ed.
      p. cm.
  Summary: When her baby sister is born too soon, Sarah does not understand what is going on until a nurse explains the tubes and wires and her mother reminds her that God is with tiny Amy, even in the hospital.
  ISBN 10: 0-310-70867-2 (hardcover)
  ISBN 13: 978-0-310-70867-4 (hardcover)
  [1. Premature babies—Fiction. 2. Babies—Hospital care—Fiction. 3. Neonatal intensive care—Fiction. 4. Sisters—Fiction. 5. Christian life—Fiction.] I. Bladholm, Cheri, ill. II. Title.
  PZ7.A4915My 2005
  [E]--dc22

                    2003027956

Zonderkidz is a trademark of Zondervan.

Editor: Amy De Vries
Art Direction & Design: Laura Maitner-Mason

Printed in China
05 06 07 08/MPH/4 3 2 1

With love to my parents,
Jo and Jerome Schmitt
Diana M. Amadeo

To the amazing "family" of models and
caring helpers for this book: Baby Ezrie Eileen O'Neill, Katia,
Holly, Betsy, Danny, Sharon, and Linda, and Katheryn Rome, R.N.
Special thanks also to the Neonatal Department of
St. Joseph's Hospital Health Center of Syracuse, New York.
Cheri Bladholm

To Rebecca Stehouwer VandeGriend, our preemie,
who has become a primo daughter, scholar, healer, wife, and mom;
and to Nancy DeVos Stehouwer for being there to make it happen.
Scott Stehouwer

It was very hard to sleep. Mommy and Daddy were making so much noise I pulled the blankets over my head.

The next thing I knew, someone touched my shoulder.

"Sarah … Sarah, it's time for school."

I pulled the covers off my head and opened my eyes. Aunt Kristi was sitting on my bed.

"Why are you here?" I asked.

"Your mommy went into labor," Aunt Kristi explained. "Her body wants to have the baby. But it's a little too early. The doctors will try some medicine to keep the baby inside."

It was hard to pay attention at school that morning. The baby wasn't supposed to come until summer. It was only spring. I was scared. I started to cry. My teacher seemed to understand. She whispered that all would be well.

It was a surprise when Daddy picked me up from school. He looked sad and very tired.

Daddy gave me a big, big kiss. "Sarah, you have a new baby sister. Her name is Amy. She's very tiny. The nurses call her a 'preemie.'"

"What's a preemie?" I asked.

"That's short for 'premature.' It means 'born too early.' Amy is very sick."

DADDY TOOK ME TO THE HOSPITAL. When I saw Mommy she smiled, but she looked a little sad too. I climbed up onto her bed and cuddled in her arms. Then, we walked to the window of the special care nursery. There were big chubby babies, skinny babies, dark and light babies. Mommy pointed to a tiny baby in a clear box. It was Amy. She was smaller than my doll!

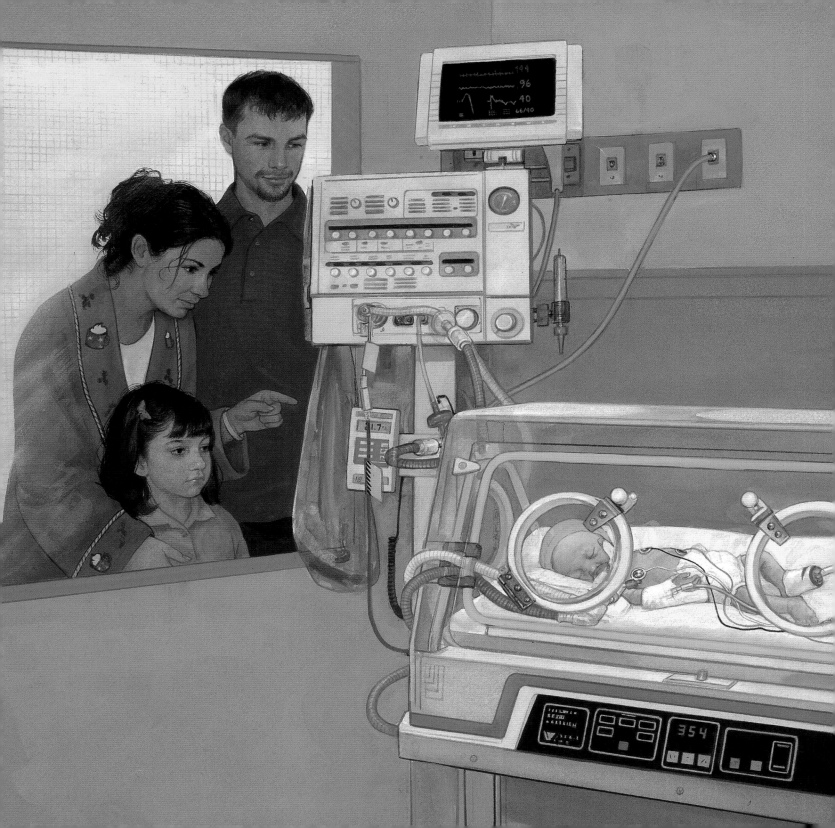

A LADY came out of the nursery. "You must be Sarah," she said, smiling. "My name is Kathryn. I'm one of the nurses taking care of your sister. Come in and meet Amy."

Kathryn took us to a sink. She showed Mommy, Daddy, and me how to scrub with a special soap. Then Kathryn gave us hospital gowns to cover our clothes. We looked funny. She led us into the nursery. It smelled clean.

Machines with red and green numbers beeped at us. When we stopped next to Amy, I could see through the clear box that she was wearing a diaper and a pink hat.

"Isn't she cold?" I asked.

"No," the nurse said. "We keep her in this heated box to watch her breathing and color."

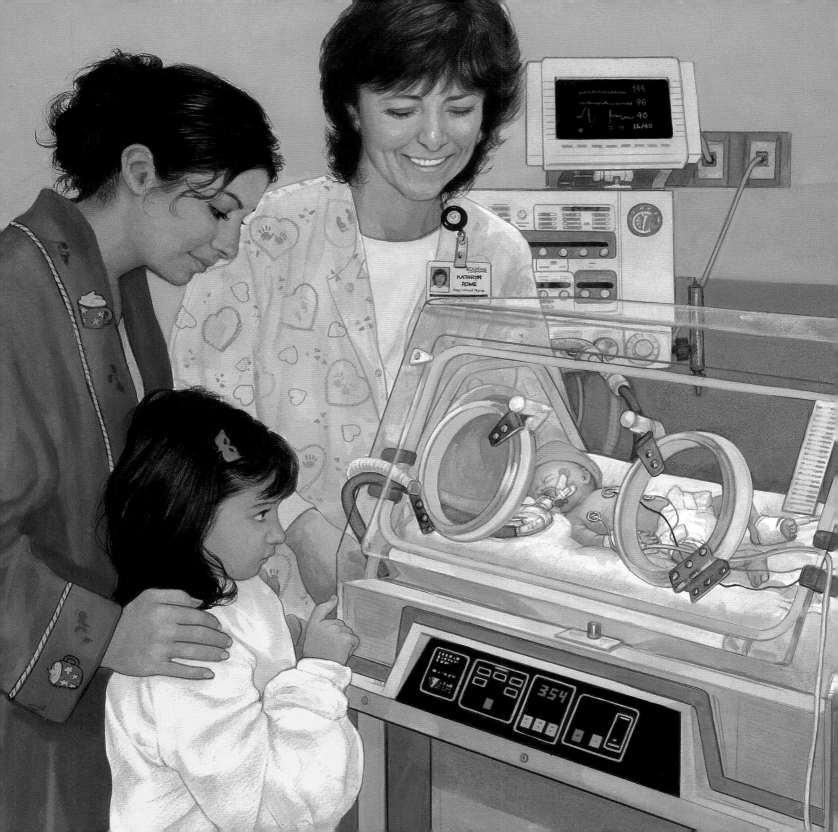

I LEANED CLOSER. Amy was asleep. Her skin was wrinkled and pink.

"What's that?" I pointed at a tube in her mouth that was hooked to a big machine.

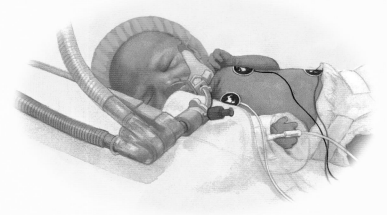

The nurse said, "When Amy forgets to breathe, the machine will do it for her."

"How can Amy eat with a tube in her throat?" I asked.

Kathryn showed me Amy's bandaged arm. "A needle in Amy's arm is connected to this tube, which comes from this plastic bag of fluid. We'll feed her through this tube until she's stronger."

"That must really hurt," I said quietly.

"We numb the areas that might feel pain," Kathryn said.

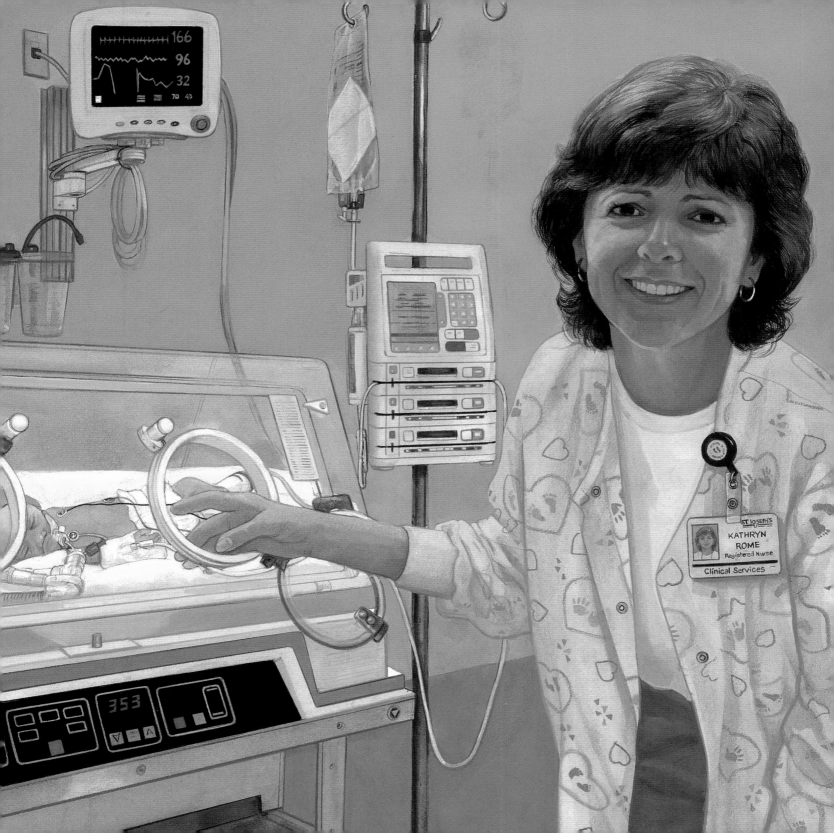

Mommy came home two days later. But things were different. When I was at school, Mommy was at the hospital with Amy. After school, she didn't listen to my stories.

"You love Amy more than me!" I shouted.

Mommy pulled me onto her lap. "You know I love you," Mommy said. "I'm just afraid."

So was I. "Is Amy going to die?"

"I don't know," Mommy said softly and hugged me tight.

"I wish I could help Amy," I said.

"You can. Pray for Amy. God is with baby Amy just like he's with us here at home."

MOMMY AND DADDY went to visit Amy all the time. At first, they were quiet and sad after each trip to the hospital. Amy didn't get better for a long time. But one day they came home wearing big smiles. Amy was better and I could finally see my baby sister again.

Amy had changed a lot since the last time I saw her. The tube was gone from her throat. The needle was out of her arm.

Kathryn said, "Amy's much better. But she's still too small to drink from a bottle. So every three hours, a nurse puts a skinny straw in Amy's mouth. Milk slides right down the straw and into her tummy. Amy will eat this way until she can suck from a bottle."

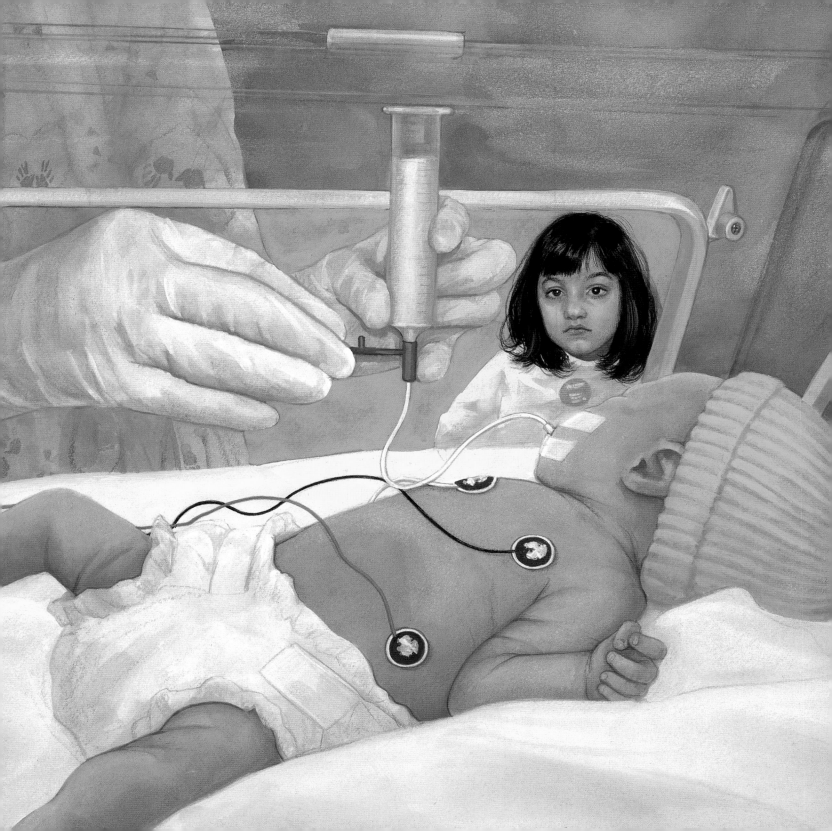

"WHAT ARE THESE?" I asked.

Amy had thin wires pasted on her chest. The wires led to a machine that had green numbers that changed each time Amy breathed. Beneath the numbers, jagged green lines of light streaked across a screen.

The nurse said, "It's called a heart-lung monitor. It keeps track of Amy's heartbeat and breathing. Now, would you like to hold Amy?"

Boy, would I!

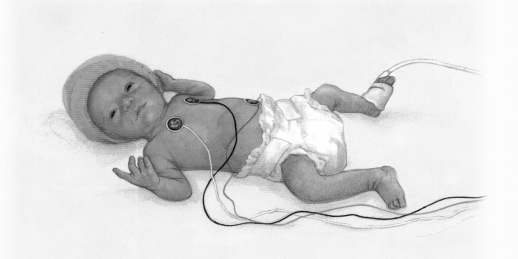

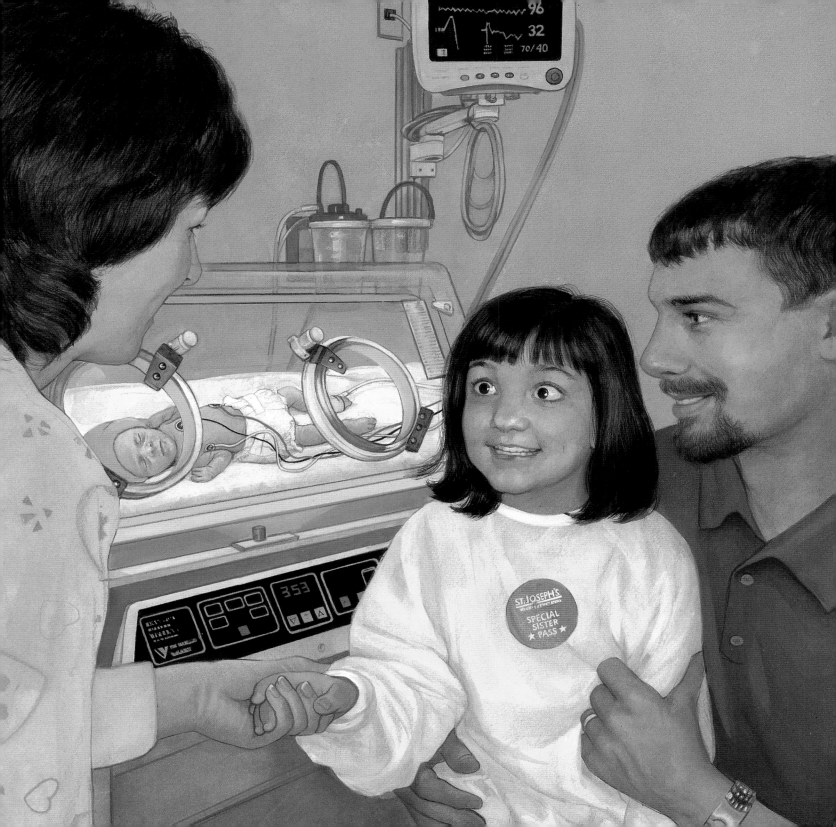

MOMMY OPENED THE TINY DOOR of the clear box. She dressed Amy in soft doll clothes and a warm knit hat. She wrapped Amy in three blankets. Then Mommy handed my sister to me.

Amy was so light! She was even lighter than my dolls! Her eyes were big and bright. The tiny bit of hair on her head was brown—just like mine!

The heart monitor sounded *beep, beep.*

The nurse took a stethoscope from around her neck and listened to Amy's heart. "Her heart is beating faster. She's excited to see you!" she said.

I didn't hold Amy long. Soon we placed her back in the warm box.

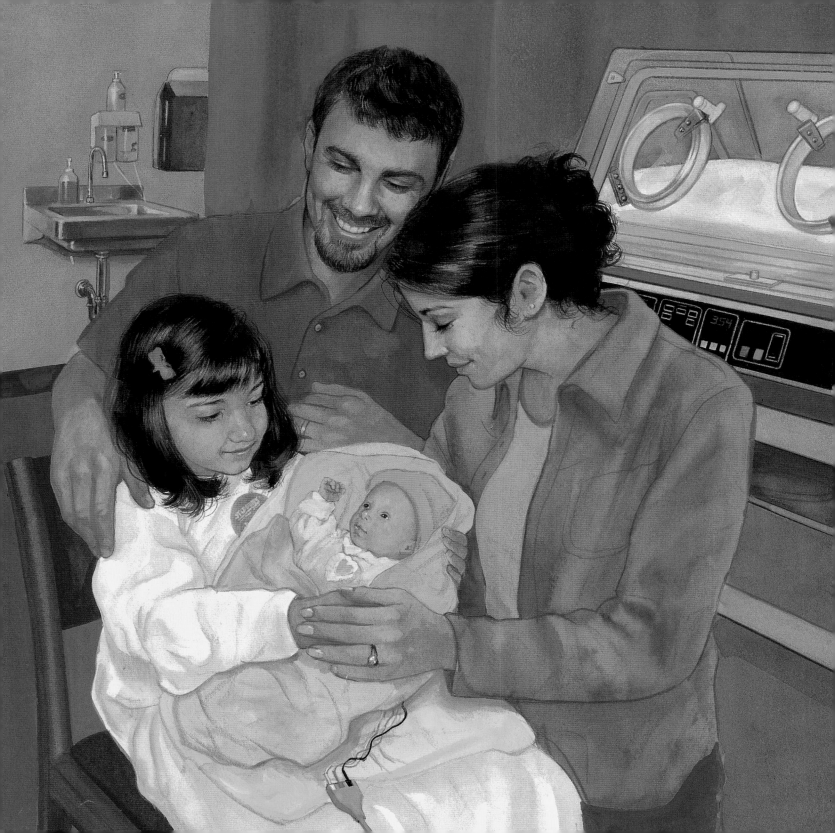

TIME PASSED QUICKLY and Amy is two months old today. She still feels light, but her cheeks are getting rounder. She has begun to suck and drink from a bottle. Soon the wires will come off her chest. When she puts on some fat, she can keep warm in a crib.

My little sister will come home soon—maybe when she gains a little more weight. I can't wait. Then we'll be all together: Mommy, Daddy, Amy, and me.

I pray, "Thank you, God, for being with Amy—even in her little box."

A Word to Parents and Other Caregivers

Children, as well as adults, struggle with a variety of feelings when faced with emotionally charged situations. By helping our children clearly recognize God's loving presence in their lives—that he is with them no matter what happens—we help to prepare them for life. One of the names of Jesus Christ is "Immanuel, God with us," and God with us is the theme of this Helping Kids Heal series. The books honestly and sensitively address the difficult emotions children face.

Children love a good story. Through stories, a child has permission to feel, to ask questions, to voice fears, and to struggle with emotions. Remember, one reading is not enough. Repetition is a great reminder of the truths taught in the story.

In the story *My Baby Sister is a Preemie*, we get a good glimpse into the world of an older sibling who struggles with the effects of a pregnancy that goes differently than expected. Sarah, the little girl in the story, shares her thoughts and feelings with her parents.

Some of the things Mom and Dad did right in this story are

1. They took time to listen to Sarah's concerns.

2. They explained what was going on with the baby. Not knowing what is happening can cause a child to expect the worst.

3. They told Sarah their own concerns for Amy. They did so without sugar-coating the situation. And they did so with a sense of optimism and in a way that was appropriate for a child her age.

4. They made sure that Sarah was included in what was going on with Amy.

The most important thing that Sarah's parents did, of course, was to remind Sarah and themselves that God was always there with all of them, including tiny Amy.

Dr. Scott

R. Scott Stehouwer, Ph.D., professor of psychology, Calvin College, and clinical psychologist